Katy Hudson

THE GOLDEN ACORN

Raintree is an imprint of Capstone
Library Limited, a company incor...
in England and Wales having its registered
office at 264 Banbury Road, Oxford, OX2
7DY – Registered company number:
6695582

www.raintree.co.uk
myorders@raintree.co.uk

ISBN 978 1 4747 7806 0
24 23 22 21 20
10 9 8 7 6 5 4 3 2 1

A full catalogue record for this book
is available from the British Library.

Printed and bound in India

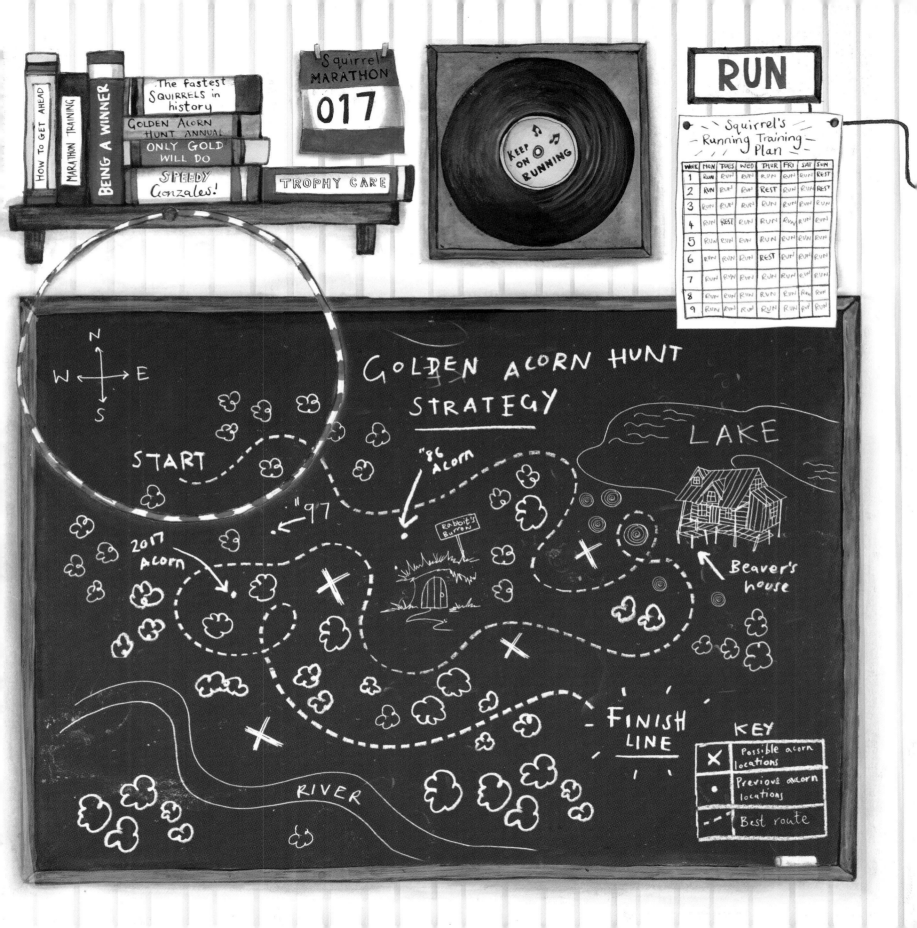

Squirrel **LOVED** being the fastest. She could
fly through the trees faster than anybody
and had the trophy collection to prove it.

Her most prized trophies were from the annual Golden Acorn Hunt.

Only the fastest racers won the Golden Acorn, and Squirrel had taken it home for the last eight years.

BUT THIS YEAR WAS DIFFERENT.

"All those competing in tomorrow's Golden Acorn Hunt must do so as part of a team," Beaver read.

Squirrel scoffed. "But I'm the fastest animal
in the forest! I don't need a team."

"But we'd love to be on your team, Squirrel!"
said Rabbit brightly.

"You?" Squirrel looked at her friends.
They really did not seem like race material.

But Squirrel had no choice. The race was tomorrow.
Maybe a little training would do the trick . . .

. . . OR MAYBE NOT.

Judge

The next morning,
Squirrel gathered her
team at the starting line.

"The Golden Acorn has been
hidden," the judge yelled.
"READY! SET! GO!"

WHOOSH! Squirrel was off, overtaking all the other racers – even her own team!

"Squirrel, wait!" her friends called. "We've lost Tortoise!"

"Ugh, Tortoise," huffed Squirrel, turning back.

Squirrel grabbed Tortoise, plopped him back on the branch, and took off again – but not for long.

"Squirrel, wait!" her friends called once more. "We're all tangled up."

Squirrel untangled her friends and was off yet again – for about ten seconds.

"You can't
be serious,"
Squirrel moaned.

"Squirrel,
wait!" her
friends called.
"Beaver is
stuck!"

"Oh, come on!"
Squirrel groaned.

Once Beaver's bottom was pushed
free, Squirrel was off as fast as her feet
would carry her – so fast that she didn't
even hear her friends calling for her.

Over logs and under branches.
Inside trunks and above treetops.
Squirrel raced as fast as she could
to find the Golden Acorn. Until . . .

It was the biggest Golden Acorn
Squirrel had ever seen! She pried it
from its hiding spot and took off.

But the Golden Acorn was heavy.
Much too heavy to carry alone.

And there was only Squirrel – all by
herself. Squirrel and her golden prize.

After lots and lots of rolling
and pushing and heaving,
she had a little rest. She
was tired and sweaty and . . .

. . . lonely.

And as Squirrel looked out at all the
other racers, still searching for the acorn,
she realized she had lost her friends.
The Golden Acorn would just have to wait.

WHOOSH! Off Squirrel raced, faster than
she ever had before. Over logs, under branches,
inside trunks and above the treetops until . . .

. . . THERE THEY WERE!

After lots and lots of rolling
and pushing and heaving,
Squirrel had her friends back.

Her team didn't come
in first, and they didn't get
a trophy. But it didn't matter.

From now on, Squirrel's friends would **ALWAYS** come first.